15626

E
Ale

Alexander, Liza
No red monsters allowed!

No Red Monsters Allowed!

By Liza Alexander
Illustrated by David Prebenna

A SESAME STREET/GOLDEN PRESS BOOK

Published by Western Publishing Company, Inc., in conjunction with Children's Television Workshop.

15626

Br-r-r-ring! Br-r-r-ring! Hazel Monster called her
friend Herry on the phone. When he answered, she
said, "Hello, Herry! Do you want to come and play in my
new tree house? I built it all by myself!"

"You bet!" said Herry. "Hannah Monster is here
visiting. Can she come, too?"

"Of course!" said Hazel. "Excellent!"

Herry and Hannah looked just like Hazel. All three of
them were blue and furry. They all had purple noses.

When Herry and Hannah arrived, Hazel's mommy made a snack for the blue monsters.

"Scrumptious," said Hannah between chomps. "This is the same snack that my mommy gives me!"

"Yeah," said Herry, slurping down his glass of carrot juice. "Celery and crunchy monster butter is the best! Thank you, Mrs. Monster!"

"Come on, Herry! Come on, Hannah!" said Hazel. "Let's go to my tree house!"

The three fuzzy blue monsters scrambled up
the ladder to Hazel's tree house.
    First they played jacks.

Next Hazel, Herry, and Hannah shot marbles.

Later, while the monsters were playing cards,
Elmo came by.

"Wow! A tree house," Elmo said. "Hazel!
Elmo wants to climb up and play."

Hazel looked down. "No way!" she said.
"No red monsters allowed!"

Elmo blushed a deeper red. He slumped to the ground. "Why can't Elmo go up to Hazel's tree house?" wondered Elmo. "Elmo can play!"

Up in the tree house, Hazel said, "Come on, everybody. Let's play cards!"

The blue monsters picked up their cards. Herry could not concentrate. He was thinking about Elmo. So was Hannah. Hannah felt like she might cry.

Then Herry spoke up. "Hazel, why can't Elmo play with us?"

"Yeah, why not?" said Hannah in a little voice. "We like Elmo."

"He can't because it's my tree house, and I say so," said Hazel. "No red monsters allowed!"

"But why not?" asked Herry. "Elmo is fun!"

Hazel thought for a moment. "Elmo can't come up and play because he's red and we're blue. Elmo is different."

"So what?" said Herry. "Red is good. Blue is good. Different is good."

Hazel thought for another moment. She liked Herry.
Herry was usually right about things.

Hazel leaned out of the tree house. "Elmo!" she called.
"I changed my mind. Climb on up."

"Yaaaay!" said Hannah.

Elmo jumped up. "Yippee! Red monsters *are* allowed!"
Up the ladder he went!

"Elmo, do you know how to play tiddlywinks?" asked Hazel.

"No," said Elmo, "but Elmo can learn."

"Sure," said Hannah. "Watch us first, and then you can play when you know how."

"Okey-dokey," said Elmo.

Elmo learned tiddlywinks right away. Even Hazel saw how much fun it was to play with both blue and red monsters.

"Now Elmo will teach you a game!" said Elmo. "It's called imagine animals! You try to guess what animal Elmo is. Here we go!"

Elmo leaned over, held his hands together, and swung his arms from side to side beneath his nose. Then he lumbered across the floor.

"Elephant!" shouted Hannah.

"Excellent!" Hazel laughed, and she and Herry clapped and cheered.

"What animal am I?" Hazel stood on her tiptoes and stretched her whole body upward so that she seemed much taller. Then she held one arm up above her head and opened and shut her hand like a mouth.

"Alligator!" said Herry.

"No, silly," said Hazel. "Look. I'm eating leaves. Munch, munch, munch."

"Horse!" said Hannah.

"No, no!" said Hazel. "Don't you get it? I'm very tall!"

"Elmo knows the answer," said Elmo. "Hazel is a giraffe!"

"That's right, Elmo!" said Hazel, and she was so excited that she gave Elmo a big hug.

"I like this game," said Hazel. "It's different."

"Are you guys hungry?" asked Elmo.

"Yes!" said all the blue monsters at once.
"Then let's go to my house for a snack!" said Elmo.
All the monsters clambered down the ladder and
over to Elmo's house.

"Hello, kids," said Elmo's furry red monster mommy. "Welcome!"

Hazel looked around. "Your house is different from ours," she said. Then she quickly added, "But your house is nice, too."

"Thank you, dear," said Elmo's mommy. She spooned fruit salad into four little bowls.

"What are these green fruits with all the seeds?" asked Herry.

"Kiwis!" said Elmo. "Yum-yum!"

"Our mommies always give us vegetables for a snack," said Hazel.

"Come on, Hazel," said Herry. "Just try it. I'm going to."

"Yes, kids, do have a taste," said Elmo's mommy. "My mother gave me kiwis when I was little. Our whole family loves them. But if you don't like kiwis, Hazel dear, you don't have to eat them."

Herry and Hannah and Hazel all took bites. Hannah and Hazel both said, "Delicious!"

"Eeeew!" said Herry. "Excuse me. I'm sorry, but I don't think I like kiwis."

Everybody laughed. "That's all right," said Elmo's mommy. "You tried them and that is what's important."

Soon it was time to go.

"Good-bye and thank you, Elmo and Mrs. Monster," said Hannah.

"Thank you very much," said Herry.

"You're welcome," said Elmo's mommy.

"Could Elmo come over to my house tomorrow, Mrs. Monster?" asked Hazel.

"Would you like that, Elmo?" asked his mommy.

"Oh, yes, Elmo would like that very much," said Elmo. "Can we play in your tree house, Hazel?"

"Sure we can," said Hazel. "Excellent! Bye, now!"

"Good-bye, Hazel! Good-bye, everybody!" called Elmo, and he and his mommy waved bye-bye.